THE NINE LIVES OF
FURRY PURRY
BEANCAT

THE
PIRATE
CAPTAIN'S
CAT

D0452315

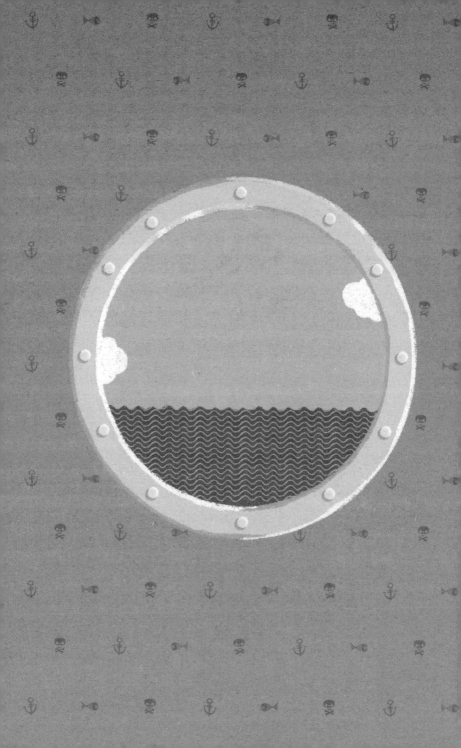

THE NINE LIVES OF
FURRY PURRY
BEANCAT

THE
PIRATE
CAPTAIN'S
CAT

PHILIP ARDAGH

Illustrated by
Rob Biddulph

SIMON & SCHUSTER

First published in Great Britain in 2020 by Simon & Schuster UK Ltd

1 3 5 7 9 10 8 6 4 2

Simon & Schuster UK Ltd
1st Floor, 222 Gray's Inn Road
London
WC1X 8HB

www.simonandschuster.co.uk

Simon & Schuster Australia, Sydney
Simon & Schuster India, New Delhi

A CIP catalogue record for this book is available from the British Library.

PB ISBN 978-1-4711-8401-7
eBook ISBN 978-1-4711-8402-4

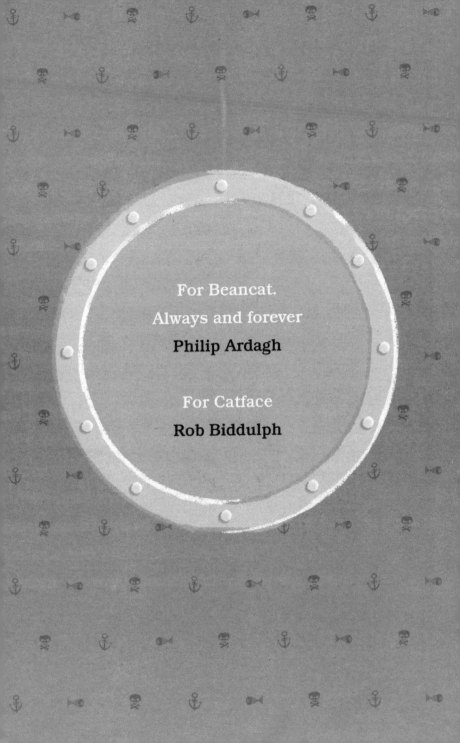

For Beancat.
Always and forever
Philip Ardagh

For Catface
Rob Biddulph

Furry Purry Beancat found a patch of sunlight, followed her tail around in a circle three times, then settled herself down in a furry ball of purry cat. She yawned, lowered her head to the ground and pulled her beautiful fluffy tail in front of her little pink nose.

Where will I wake up next? she wondered, slowly closing her big green eyes and drifting off to sleep . . .

CHAPTER 1
'ALL ABOARD!'

Furry Purry Beancat opened her big green eyes to find that she was sitting on top of a pirate captain's hat. She peered down to discover that the pirate captain's hat was on top of a pirate captain's HEAD.

That makes sense, she thought, but *what a strange place to—*

Just then, a large cannonball went whistling past her beautiful ears.

Weeeeeeeeeeeeeeeeeeeeeee!

'PREPARE TO REPEL ALL BOARDERS!' shouted the pirate captain, whatever that meant. His deep voice boomed up through the hat and through Beancat's furry, purry body.

The captain reached up, scooped up Furry Purry Beancat and put her down on the ship's deck behind a barrel marked

SHIP'S BISCUITS.

'You'll be safe here, Beancat,' he said.

Safer, thought Beancat, *but probably not as safe as if I were curled up in a*

cat basket in the corner of a creamery! I wonder where I am now?

This was all *very* exciting for her who, before falling asleep earlier that day, had been somewhere completely and utterly different. You see, Furry Purry Beancat isn't just your average cat. Oh no. Because Beancat often falls asleep in one place and time, and then wakes up somewhere completely new! Wherever an adventure needs her, that's where Beancat will be. And now it seemed adventure was calling on the high seas!

The pirate captain's hands were big and hairy but he'd been as gentle as gentle can be when he'd taken Furry Purry Beancat from the top of his head.

Now THERE'S a man who knows how to treat a cat, she thought. *He must be my human, which means that I'm a pirate captain's cat! How excit–*

Another cannonball went whizzing by – **Weeeeeeeeeeeeeeeeeeeeee!** – narrowly missing the ship's wheel this time, and crashing into a railing at the far edge of the deck, causing it to splinter into the sea.

A pirate toppled after it, to cries of, 'MAN OVERBOARD!'

Now, Furry Purry Beancat certainly knew what THAT meant. She jumped up on to the barrel of ship's biscuits for a better view. She saw another ship alongside this one, and people leaping across the gap between the two. Some of them were swinging across on ropes.

Wherever I am, it seems I've arrived in the middle of the action! thought Furry Purry Beancat.

The attackers were shouting at the top of their voices, trying to look and sound as frightening as possible. There was the **FLASH-BANG** of firing flintlock pistols, puffs of smoke and the endless **THUD** of boots and shoes and bare feet landing on the deck.

Furry Purry Beancat did a really big cat yawn, one where you could see the roof of her mouth, with teeth bared like a tiger: *YAAAAAAAAAAWN!*

It seemed to say, *If you're trying to*

impress me, you're not doing a very good job at it.

Furry Purry Beancat is VERY good at cat yawns.

The pirate captain charged away to face the invaders of his ship, cutlass in hand, his scarlet coat flowing behind him as he ran. The coat looked as if it must have been very fine once, but Beancat's beady cat eyes picked out the fact that the coat's gold brocade was frayed and that a good many buttons were missing.

The captain had a pair of flintlock pistols tucked into his belt, his jet-black hair in a ponytail, and a great big grin on his face when he turned to look back and saw Beancat on the barrel.

'Defend the *Rapier* to the death!' he commanded.

The Rapier *must be the name of this ship,* thought Beancat. *And what a great pirate captain my pirate captain makes!* She watched him join the battle that had begun on deck. Well, perhaps 'battle' wasn't exactly right . . . There was plenty of fighting, but it didn't seem to be very well organized at all!

There must be something I can do to help! Beancat thought. *This is my ship and he's my captain!*

'You'd better get down from there if you don't want your ears blown off, Beancat!' said a voice above the din of clashing swords, wild shouts and punches. The voice was thick and rich, like treacle.

Furry Purry Beancat looked to her left, to her right, then up, then—

'Down here, you numbskull!' said the voice. 'It's me! Gordon.'

She looked down on to the deck. A beady-eyed rat was looking up at her. He had beautiful glossy dark-brown fur – not as beautiful as Beancat's fur, of course – and a mischievous twinkle in his eyes.

Now there's a surprise! thought Beancat. *A cat and a rat.* She jumped down next to Gordon. *And, by the way he's talking, we must be friends!*

'Let's hide in here,' said the rat, hopping into the middle of a large coil of rope. 'We should still get a good view.'

Furry Purry Beancat jumped in next to him. 'What's going on?' she asked. She wanted to know who was attacking and why.

'Watcha mean, what's going on?' asked Gordon. 'We're under attack, Beancat!'

'Yes, but I was having a cat nap on the captain's hat,' Furry Purry Beancat explained, 'so I missed the start of it all.'

'Typical!' Gordon grinned, showing a neat row of ratty teeth.

'Dunno why Captain Topaz lets you get away with it!'

So, his name is Topaz, thought Furry Purry Beancat, storing away the information.

Both animals fell silent and peered over the top of the rope to watch the fighting.

Furry Purry Beancat tried to think about what she knew about pirates, apart from the skull-and-crossbones flag and treasure maps, of course. *They attack ships, take prisoners and steal chests of gold . . .*

'Who are they, Gordon?' asked Furry Purry Beancat.

Gordon gave her a funny look.

'Why are you looking at me like that?' she asked.

'Are you havin' another one of your

forget-it-all moments?' asked Gordon. 'Who do you think's attacking us? The Archbishop of Canterbury or One-Eyed Bart?'

Furry Purry Beancat watched Captain Topaz clashing swords with one of the attackers. The man was wearing a similar coat to the captain's but it was black rather than scarlet. He had a patch over where his left eye would be . . . 'One-Eyed Bart!' she cried.

'Correct!' said Gordon. 'Give the cat a fish!'

Furry Purry Beancat could tell that both Bart and Captain Topaz were very good swordsmen. The clanking of cutlass against cutlass was loud and went on for a

long time. Meanwhile, the other members
of the two pirate crews were fighting each
other every which way!

Furry Purry Beancat watched pirates:

- wrestling
- punching
- chasing each other with clubs
- throwing anything and everything
  they could find
- running after each other up and
  down the rigging

This looked truly DANGEROUS!

She could just make out a pirate, up
in the crow's nest at the very top of the
tallest mast, wearing a red bandanna with

white spots on his head.

He was dropping coconuts on One-Eyed Bart's men and he appeared to have a good supply!

The loud **TOCK!**s of coconuts coming into contact with human heads, followed by the cries from the poor pirates, were enough to make Furry Purry Beancat swivel her ears in the opposite direction!

'What say we go somewhere quieter?' said Gordon.

'And safer,' said Furry Purry Beancat. 'Good idea!'

Gordon didn't need asking twice. He dashed off. As she followed, Beancat noticed that the end of the rat's tail was missing from what looked like an old injury, long healed.

They darted past battling pirates including the two ships' cooks: one armed with a metal ladle and the other a huge wooden spoon!

Furry Purry Beancat had spotted them earlier. They'd been using the kitchen utensils like swords, but now they'd switched to hitting each other over the head with them instead.

CLUNK! 'Ouch!'

THWACK! 'Ooof!'

Gordon suddenly took a flying jump and disappeared down an open hatch.

Without a second thought, Furry Purry Beancat followed him, leaping into the depths of the ship. As she fell through

the air, she turned over a few times –
rather gracefully, in fact – her beautiful
fur all fluffed up. She ended with her
party trick of turning upright just in time
so she hit the ground – well, *deck* in this
case – paws-first.

Furry Purry Beancat felt good inside,
proud of her balletic manoeuvres!

She looked around the lower deck.
Everything seemed much more peaceful
here. Empty hammocks swung gently
with the movement of the water. They were
obviously sailing on a calm sea; quite a
contrast to all the clattering and banging
and shouting going on above deck.

'Oh, there you are, Gordon!' said a
relieved rat in a shaky voice, peering out

from under a piece of sacking in a shadowy corner. 'I was beginning to get worried.'

'You worry about EVERYTHING, Ethel,' said Gordon. 'It's just not rat-like!'

As Ethel stepped into the light, Furry Purry Beancat saw that she looked very like Gordon – the same beautiful, brown fur – except she was a little smaller and had a full-length tail. 'Hello, FPBC!' she said.

'Hi, Ethel,' said Furry Purry Beancat, having heard her name from Gordon. She tried to sound as casual and *of-course-I-know-who-you-are* as possible. It was second nature for her to pretend to be at home wherever she awoke!

'Where are the kids?' Gordon asked Ethel, looking around, his eyes adjusting to the darker corners after the bright sunshine up above.

'I thought we should take advantage of the distraction on deck to search the kitchen for food,' said Ethel proudly. 'I've sent all eight of them there.'

'Alone?' Gordon gasped.

'No, not alone!' said Ethel. 'Of course not! I sent them with Uncle Morris.'

Gordon's eyes widened. 'You put your bruvver, Morris, in charge of the kids? He couldn't k—'

Just then, a man came falling through the open hatch in the ceiling – which was the floor of the deck above – and landed on the floor, far less gracefully than Gordon or Furry Purry Beancat.

THUD!

'Ooof!' he groaned. 'Aaargh.' Next, he rubbed the back of his head. 'Ouch!' Then he struggled to his feet.

'I'll get you, you—!' The pirate proceeded to say a VERY rude word (which made Ethel blush beneath her fur) as he shook his fist up at the open hatch to the person, out of Beancat's view, who'd knocked him down there. He hobbled over to the wooden steps leading up and out of the hatch that Beancat and Gordon had jumped through – more ladder than staircase – and made his way back up to the main deck.

'Let's hope Morris is in one of his more sensible moods,' said Gordon, under his breath. 'He'll need his wits about him in this free-for-all.'

Suddenly, there was a loud **BOOM** from above.

Furry Purry Beancat began cleaning the white of her front paws (as cats often do after a bit of a shock). Because she has such long fur, she had to turn her head to one side and then turn it back again with her tongue out to get in a really good, long lick. Furry Purry Beancat is particularly proud of her four white paws.

Gordon and Ethel must be married, she thought as she washed. *With LOTS of children.*

'Do you think this is serious?' asked Ethel. Taking Beancat's lead, she began washing her nose and whiskers with her tiny front paws. Furry Purry Beancat suspected that this too was more of a worry-wash than a proper clean. After all, there was plenty to worry about!

There was a distant explosion and the ship tremored.

'What do you reckon, Beancat?' Gordon asked, turning to her.

Furry Purry Beancat stopped cleaning mid-lick and put her paw back on the lower-deck floor. 'Captain Topaz has been the captain of this ship for as long as I can remember,' she said, which was true. Even if that 'for as long as' was only since waking up on his head! 'And I don't think he'll be giving up being captain any time soon.'

'That's the spirit!' said Gordon.

'But I think it's important we do all WE can to help him and the crew,' she added. 'This ship is our home too!'

In the background, behind their conversation, was the constant sound of fighting from up above.

THUNK!

BING!

BISH!

BASH!

BOSH!

Just then a boy, wearing little more

than rags, ran down the wooden steps in bare feet. He was streaked in dirt all over; so much so that it was impossible to tell what colour his hair actually was underneath it all.

Neither nervous Ethel nor Gordon moved.

This surprised Furry Purry Beancat (though she was careful not to show it). Surely ship's rats weren't popular with the sailors? Shouldn't they hide. . . and fast?

CHAPTER 2
FRIENDS AND ENEMIES

The boy came over to the shadows and gave Furry Purry Beancat a quick stroke. 'Ahoy there, Beancat!' he said. 'Keeping out of the way of all this?' He jerked his head in the direction of the deck above. 'Right sensible.'

He seems nice, thought Beancat. *Even*

if he does smell like a pedal bin. She suspected pirates didn't get to wash that much unless they jumped into the sea. *And I wonder where I remember the smell of a pedal bin from?* she pondered.

The boy picked up Gordon carefully and rubbed him between the ears. 'Ahoy there, Gordon!' he said lovingly.

'Greetin's, Powder Monkey!' said the rat, though, of course, all the boy heard were ratty squeaks because he couldn't speak Animal. But at least Beancat now knew the boy's name.

'Can't stop,' said Powder Monkey, putting Gordon down. 'I'm on a mission!' He ran over to one of the hammocks and began rummaging under a grey blanket which had been repaired so many times that it looked more like a patchwork quilt. 'First Mate Muggins needs this!' he said triumphantly, as he pulled something from underneath the blanket. 'It's his lucky charm!'

If Furry Purry Beancat had been given all the time in the world, she would never have guessed in a million years – *two* million years – what Powder Monkey was holding.

It was black and hideous, leathery and . . . and horrible! It looked like a very small monkey but with a fish's tail instead of back legs.

Beancat sniffed the air and gave a look of total disapproval (you know, the sort

of face a cat gives you when it's been pestering you to feed it but, when you *do* it looks at the food and then an expression which suggests, 'You can't expect me to eat THAT!').

What on earth is that thing? she wondered. *It smells even worse than Powder Monkey. Does the first mate snuggle up with it in his hammock like a child with a teddy bear?*

Powder Monkey clutched the ugly object tightly as he dashed back up the stairs.

'Oh dear!' said Ethel, doing another worry-wash. 'If First Mate Muggins wants his mermaid, things must be serious.'

Mermaid? thought Beancat. *Aren't*

mermaids supposed to be graceful and beautiful and human-sized, not like a shrunken monkey someone has stuck a tail to?

'Don't go worryin' yourself, Ethel,' said Gordon. 'Muggins is a fine fighter and with his lucky charm, he'll be a better fighter still!'

'You don't believe in all that, do you?' Beancat asked him.

'That ain't the point, is it?' said Gordon. 'It's whether Muggins believes it that matters.'

Good point! thought Furry Purry Beancat. *Now to join the fight!*

But she had no time to think any more about it because a plump, grey rat – with one ear and just about the goofiest expression she had ever seen on any animal – came bumbling into view, quickly followed by seven young rats, tumbling over each other in excitement.

'Here we all are!' said the one-eared rat.

This must be Morris! thought Beancat.

Ethel did a quick head count then looked again. 'Where's Blue?' she said, the panic sounding in her voice.

'Stuck down a hole!' said one young rat, with a laugh.

'Trapped under a barrel!' cried another.

'Squashed by the cook!'

'Eaten by a rat-eater!'

'Fell overboard!'

'Cut into tiny little pieces!'

'Drowning in a bowl of stew!'

'Who's Blue?' asked the one-eared rat v-e-r-y s-l-o-w-l-y.

'WHO'S BLUE?' cried Gordon. 'What do you mean, who's—?'

'Here I am, Dad!' said the eighth young rat, finally putting in an appearance. This rat was noticeably smaller than her brothers and sisters and her fur was a gorgeous black. She was speaking with her mouth full because she was carrying a piece of string.

'Oh, THAT Blue,' said the goofy grey rat, with a grin. 'She's right there.' He pointed with a claw, as though he'd known where Blue was ALL the time. 'I knew Blue was there *all* the time,' he added.

See? I told you.

'You don't say,' said Gordon but, truth be told, he looked DELIGHTED. 'Good girl!' he said to Blue. 'You can never have too much string!' He turned to her siblings. 'You shouldn't go worrying us like that.'

'So-rry, Dad!' said all seven together, in one sing song voice. Next, they turned to Ethel, who was looking mighty relieved. 'So-rry, Mamma!'

They formed a circle around Gordon, tumbling over each other again.

'Who's winning, Dad?'

'Has Captain Topaz poked out One-Eyed Bart's other eye yet?'

'Is there lots of blood?'

'Did you get to BITE any of the enemy?'

'Did any of the attackers drop any FOOD?'

'Has anyone fired a cannon?'

'Has anyone been pushed overboard?'

'All right, Miss Beancat?' asked Blue, quietly appearing at her side.

Furry Purry Beancat looked down at the little, black rat. 'Yes, thank you, Blue. . . Good work with the string,' she added, though in all honesty, she wasn't really sure what use little lengths of string would be.

'Thank you,' said Blue. Beancat could

hear the pride in the little rat's voice. 'I
have very important news!'

'What is it?' asked Beancat, but her
question was drowned out by Gordon.

'Anything to report, Morris?' asked
Gordon.

The goofy one-eared rat thought before answering. 'Hmmm!' he said slowly.

'HMMMMMM!' said Blue's brothers and sisters, copying him.

'Show your uncle some respect!' Ethel insisted.

'So-rry, Mamma!' said the seven naughty rats.

'Dad! I have news!' said Blue, more urgently this time.

Ethel prodded the one-eared rat with her nose. 'Well?' she asked. 'What did you see?'

'You were right, Ethel,' said Morris at long last. 'There was no one in the kitchen because it was all paws on deck!'

'All HANDS on deck,' Gordon corrected

him. 'They're humans, remember.'

The seven young rats fell about laughing.

'All paws on deck! All paws on deck!'

'Shush!' said Gordon sternly.

They all shushed. Except for Blue. 'Dad!' she said. AGAIN.

'So, was there plenty of food lying around?' her father asked their uncle.

Morris thought again before answering. 'No,' he said at last.

Furry Purry Beancat is, like most cats, a BIG fan of food – as I've already said – but she did think that they might be spending their time better *helping her captain!* She was about to say as much when—

'Not a crumb!' said a little rat.

'Not a weevil!'

'Not a fish scale!'

'Not so much as a seahorse!' said one.

'Not so much as a real HORSE!' said another.

They fell about laughing again, but not Blue.

'Not so much as a whale's tail!' cried one.

More laughter.

'Not so much as a whale's BOTTOM!' shouted the naughtiest of the naughty little rats.

There was silence. They looked from their mother to their father. Had they gone too far?

Then Gordon burst out laughing, so they ALL ended up laughing. Even Ethel! But still not Blue.

'DAD!' said the littlest rat for the umpteenth time. 'I have VERY IMPORTANT NEWS!'

They would probably have found out what it was there and then, if a group of pirates hadn't suddenly swarmed down from the upper deck.

Strange pirates.

Unfamiliar pirates.

Below decks on *THEIR* ship.

These were members of One-Eyed Bart's crew! And they looked VERY pleased with themselves.

'Search every corner! If there are any

of Captain Topaz's snivelling, lily-livered cowardly crew hiding out here, we'll find 'em!' snapped the one who seemed to be in charge: a mean-looking man with a huge scar on one side of his face. (Although, of course, there are plenty of VERY NICE PEOPLE who have scars on their faces, this man was clearly NOT VERY NICE at all. There are also very nice people with just one eye, come to that. But that should go without saying.)

'Aye, sir!' the others chanted.

The pirates started flinging aside the bedclothes in the hammocks and any bundles of blankets or clothing which might be hiding someone.

'Look! A mangy cat!' said one with not a

single hair atop his shiny, sunburned head. He made to snatch Furry Purry Beancat by the scruff of her neck.

This was not a wise move because Furry Purry Beancat can turn into *Scratchy Bitey* Beancat in the blink of an eye. Especially when called 'mangy', which is not a very polite thing to call anyone.

Before the bald pirate could say, 'What's this cat doing wrapped around my head, biting my nose, with all four claws stuck into the back of my head?' Beancat had wrapped herself around his head, biting his nose, with all four claws stuck into the back of his head.

Not only was this very painful for the pirate, he couldn't see where he was

going. He blundered about, shouting, 'Get this thing off me!'

His crewmates tried to help but there wasn't much they could do, especially when Beancat simply held on tighter! *Thing*, indeed!

At this stage, Gordon thought it would be a good time to help Beancat. He gave the order, 'ANKLES!' and he, all eight of his children, Ethel and Uncle Morris launched themselves at Bart's crew.

'Ouch!

'Argh!'

'Aroooh!'

'No!'

'AAARRHHH!'

The enemy didn't know what was

happening at first. Especially the man who had a cat on his face and could see nothing but Beancat's furry tum-tum VERY close up!

It was only when One-Eyed Bart's crew made the wise decision to flee back into the open air that Beancat finally let go of the pirate's head, dropped through the open hatch and landed – right side-up, of course – at the bottom of the stairs.

'Good work, Beancat!' said Ethel.

'Good work, *everyone!*' said Beancat with a purr, for she was, indeed, Furry Purry Beancat once more. And she was ready for ACTION! 'Now,' she asked. 'What is this important news you want to tell us, Blue?'

CHAPTER 3
PRISONER!

Things may have seemed to be going fine for Furry Purry Beancat and the rats in their little corner of the ship, but sadly the same could not be said for the rest of Captain Topaz's crew aboard the *Rapier*.

A rapier is a light, sharp-pointed sword, ideal for a quick thrust and cut,

so is an excellent name for a pirate ship: quick in the water, quick to attack, and quick to be off and out of it when the deed is done.

Except that the *Rapier* was now at anchor and its crew defeated.

Outnumbered and out-gunned by One-Eyed Bart and his men, the *Rapier* crew had been led to the hold, many of them with their hands or legs tied with rope. The hold was a large, deep, dark, windowless space low down in the hull, usually used for storing cargo. It now acted as a heavily-guarded dungeon with nothing but sacks for company. Even poor Powder Monkey had now been captured.

'Well, shiver me timbers!' said

Gordon, as the animals crouched together by the ship's wheel as night began to fall. 'I never thought I'd live to see the day when Captain Topaz was defeated . . . and aboard his own vessel too!'

I wanted us to join the action but they're already OUT of action, thought Furry Purry Beancat. And then there was Blue's important news: she'd overheard Bart planning to SINK THE SHIP.

Captain One-Eyed Bart's ship was moored up alongside them, with bridges of planks lashed between the two. Once they had loaded the treasure onto their ship, they'd separate the two and sink the *Rapier*.

'Do you think we'd find friendly rats aboard the *Pantaloon*?' Uncle Morris asked as the animals watched the enemy pirates carry their bounty of kegs of rum and brandy, fine silks and trinkets across the planks and on to the other ship.

'The what?' asked Gordon.

'The *Pantaloon*.'

Whose pantaloons?' asked Gordon. (Pantaloons are baggy trousers, so he had NO idea what Morris was going on about.)

Why would there be friendly rats down someone's baggy trousers? Furry Purry Beancat wondered. It makes no SENSE. But, then again, I suspect Ethel's brother Morris rarely makes sense!

'The ship! One-Eared Bob's ship! The *Pantaloon!*' said Morris, as if Gordon were the silly one.

'Not One-Eared Bob, One-*Eyed Bart!*' said an exasperated Gordon. 'And it's not the *Pantaloon*, you numbskull! It's the *Doubloon*! Like the gold coins! Honestly!'

Furry Purry Beancat watched more and more of the *Rapier's* cargo being moved to the enemy vessel. *They're taking it all before they sink us*, she thought. *We've got to find a way to stop them and, with all of the crew being held prisoner, it's down to us.*

'Come on, Gordon, let's track down Captain Topaz!' she said, suddenly getting to her feet. 'Let's go!'

Together, they darted here and there, between the legs of pirates, up, down, above, below, across and sideways. And there was no sign of him.

'Where can he have got to?' said Gordon at last.

'He's in his cabin with One-Eyed Bart!' squeaked little Blue, popping up between them. 'I just spied them there!'

'Well done, me little princess!' said
Gordon, his voice full of pride and praise.

'*And* I found another piece of string!'
she added proudly.

'Is there no end to your talent?' said
her father.

Is there no end to the string? Beancat
wondered.

Somehow, Furry Purry Beancat knew
Captain Topaz's cabin was at the back (or
'stern' in nautical talk) of the ship on the
main deck. Was it instinct, perhaps? She

began to make her way across the deck,
alone, leaping from barrel to railing to
deck to—

Ooops!

Beancat landed four-square on a dozing
drunken pirate's tummy, with the bounce
of a quality mattress. He opened one

bleary eye. 'What a priddy puddytat!' he said, hiccupped, then went straight back to sleep.

ZZZZzzzzzzzzZZZZ.

Phew! That was close! thought Beancat.

She liked to work alone when she could, moving at her own pace, being a shadow when she needed, a *beeeeautiful* cat when she wanted and she could think on her feet.

She continued weaving her way along the deck until she reached a thick wooden door studded with nails. It was not just firmly shut but also guarded by a pirate with a neck as wide as a tree trunk.

She came to a halt. This was Captain

Topaz's cabin, she was sure of it. But how could she get past the guard? She darted up and across the upper deck (which was also the roof of the cabin), hoping to find another way in. With so much going on, no one paid much attention to a cat darting about the place.

Reaching the very back of the ship, she stuck her beautiful furry head through a gap in the balustrading at the edge and peered down.

There was a long drop to the sea. Beancat stretched her neck out as far as she could. The back of the captain's cabin appeared to be a series of big windows made up of small diamond-shaped panes of glass, held together with strips of lead, making an overall mesh pattern. There was a narrow wooden windowsill running the length of the windows.

The problem is, Furry Purry Beancat thought, *even if I could jump down, grab hold of the windowsill, dig in my claws and pull myself up, there's no guarantee Captain Topaz would or could let me in and, if not, there's no way I can jump back up here again.*

But, really, her BIGGEST fear was that if she jumped and missed the ledge, she'd fall straight into the sea. And, if there's one thing Furry Purry Beancat HATES, it's getting wet. Not only that, she'd probably drown, which wouldn't be much help to her OR to Captain Topaz!

No, she would need a different plan to get inside the cabin.

Pulling her head back through the bars, she darted across the upper deck and back down to the main deck. Furry Purry Beancat raised her very fine and very fluffy tail and walked to the mighty man guarding the cabin.

She swished her tail like a proud peacock flashing his tail feathers. She made the most of that short distance. She was like a model on a – er – catwalk. Everything about her screamed, *Aren't I the most beautiful, gorgeous cat you've ever had the HONOUR to set your eyes upon?*

She gave the politest meow: 'Meow.'

See? And then she began rubbing her stupendously soft fur against his legs, purring like only Furry Purry Beancat can.

The face of the guard, whose arm muscles were thicker than party balloons, but a whole lot harder, broke into a smile to reveal he had just three teeth, all of which were made of gold. He bent down and, with a hand the size of a dinner-plate, he patted Furry Purry Beancat on the back like someone who'd never really petted a pet before.

'Who's a handsome boy?' he asked in a voice as deep as the ocean.

'*Meow!*'

What Beancat was saying was, '*Actually, I'm a beautiful girl, not a handsome boy,*'

not that she expected him to understand.

Obviously delighted to discover just how furry and purry Furry Purry Beancat was, the mountain of a man tried giving her a proper stroke and, having such big hands, found that he was rather good at it. Furry Purry Beancat rather liked it too.

'I wonder what your name is,' said the pirate.

'And I wonder what yours is,' meowed Beancat.

'I'm Ten-Tun,' said Ten-Tun, which gave Furry Purry Beancat quite the shock for a moment. Could the man understand Animal? 'I'm called Ten-Tun on account of the fact that I can lift ten tuns – ten barrels – filled with rum at the same time,' he told the cat proudly. And, given she had not asked for this information, Beancat assumed his previous answer to her question had been a fluke.

Ten-Tun picked up Furry Purry Beancat – who made no attempt to bite or scratch or claw because she wanted him to LIKE her – and looked at her, face to face, his piercing light blue eyes looking deep into

her green ones. 'Wait a minute. You ain't a he-cat,' the pirate said. 'You're a she-cat, ain't you? And a 'strodinarily beautiful one at that!'

He held Beancat to his enormous chest. With her great big cat ears and cat senses, she could hear Ten-Tun's heart thumping away.

'My real name is Tommy,' he whispered. 'But that's our secret. It don't sound right for a pirate, somehow.'

And Furry Purry Beancat knew that, although Ten-Tun was officially the enemy and keeping Captain Topaz hostage, even if she could suddenly be understood by humans, she would never tell anyone his secret. There are things a person can tell an animal – a cat, a dog, a rabbit, a hamster, a mouse, a guinea pig or even a goldfish – that are spoken in trust and remain private, as part of a sacred bond.

He put her back down on the deck and she sat at his feet. This made him very happy.

Now that Ten-Tun and Furry Purry Beancat were firm friends, all she could do was wait: wait until the door opened to let someone in or out, and then she would *ziiiiiiiiip* straight inside without so much as a by your leave. Beancat had planned to make the guard like her, whoever he might be. It was all part of the plan. What she HADN'T expected was to like him so much in return. She rubbed around his ankles and strained to listen at the door, hoping to pick out the faintest sounds of conversation from within.

The wood wasn't as thick as Ten-Tun's muscles but it was thick enough to turn any conversation on the other side of it into nothing more than mumbles, even to Furry Purry Beancat's super cat ears.

As she strained to hear what was going on inside the cabin, Beancat caught the sound of footsteps on the other side of the door. Footsteps that seemed to be getting louder and therefore, she assumed, closer . . .

This could be her chance.

Beneath her fluffy fur, Beancat's heart began to beat a little faster.

Any minute now . . .

The door opened, and out stepped One-Eyed Bart.

Although interested in the enemy, Furry Purry Beancat didn't waste a moment to stop and study him. She dashed between the legs of Ten-Tun and Bart into the cabin. Moments later, the door slammed shut behind her.

If she had expected Captain Topaz to look downcast and defeated, she was in for a surprise. Instead, he sat behind his desk as though he were still commanding his ship. His right hand was darkened with gunpowder from firing his flintlock pistol. His left hand was bandaged with a kerchief. His face broke into a grin when he saw Furry Purry Beancat.

'There you are, my faithful girl!' he said.

She jumped up on to the desk in front of him, landing on a sea chart and he stroked her furry body with his good hand.

She *purrrrrrrrrrrrrred*.

'Bart will pay for what he's done today!' said the captain, 'but if he or any of his crew had laid a hand on you –' the captain paused, '– their punishment would have been worse still!'

He stood and picked up Beancat, holding her in his left arm and stroking her head as he spoke.

'A prisoner in my own cabin, with my

weapons taken from me and – more to the point, my furry, purry friend – Bart's taken anything I might *use* as a weapon,

too . . . Yet escape I must, and escape I will!'

Captain Topaz stood facing the windows at the back of his cabin, looking out from the stern of the ship to the sea and sky beyond.

'Yes, I could climb through a window and dive into the sea. But abandon the *Rapier* and my crew and, worst of all, you?' He looked down at Beancat and scratched her between the ears.

Purrrrrrrrrrrrrrrr. That felt so GOOD.

'Never!' he said.

The pirate captain threw himself on to a three-legged stool, which promptly broke, causing the pair of them crash to the floor. Beancat jumped safely from his arms and landed on a large globe which started spinning.

She had to run on the spot to stop herself falling off, causing the globe to spin faster, forcing her to run faster still.

Watching from the floor, the captain laughed and laughed and laughed.

Furry Purry Beancat launched herself free of the globe and landed at his side.

'It is so VERY good to see you,' said Captain Topaz, chuckling as he got back on his feet. He studied the broken stool. 'That,' he said, when he saw that the seat of the stool was riddled with tiny holes, 'is one very bad case of woodworm.' Furry Purry Beancat knew what woodworm were: tiny little creatures that eat wood.

Luckily, they take their time because quick-eating woodworm aboard an all-wooden ship would NOT be good news.

With her super-sensitive swivelling cat ears, Beancat was sure she heard a tiny little giggle from inside the stool, followed by a *Munch! Munch! Munch!* which is a very tiny, *Munch! Munch! Munch!*

'It turns out these little worms may have done us a mighty favour!' said Captain Topaz. He was holding one of the stool legs in his hand, which now looked like a large wooden club. It was the sort of wooden club that one pirate might use to bop another pirate over the head with, when making a daring escape!

If I wanted an adventurous life, I've

landed myself in one this time around, thought Beancat. *If only Captain Topaz could speak Cat, I'd be able to tell him One-Eyed Bart is planning to sink this ship!*

CHAPTER 4
'NO WAY OUT?'

Now, it goes without saying that hitting another person over the head with the leg of a woodworm-riddled stool is Not A Good Thing. But this is PIRATES we're talking about and, as Furry Purry Beancat had herself realized by now, real-life pirates and story pirates are two very

different kinds of people. Real pirates are thieves, robbers and bandits! So hitting one another over the head wasn't that unexpected.

Furry Purry Beancat jumped on to the curved lid of a large wooden chest as her captain sat back down at his desk.

'Lucky that we buried all our gold back on that island, isn't it, Beancat?' he said, nodding at the chest. 'I'd hate that blaggard One-Eyed Bart to get his thieving hands on it. Right now he may have my ship, my crew, my weapons and all my keys, but he won't steal my treasure! And he's not won yet! We've sailed the seven seas together, Beancat, and I'm not going to let it end like this!'

Furry Purry Beancat purred. Pirate or no pirate, Captain Topaz was HER pirate captain and it was obvious that they'd been on lots of adventures together. And, just as importantly (if not MORE importantly), he loved her to bits.

She plonked her furry, purry, plump body on a sea chart. The captain reached out and rubbed her under the chin.

'We find ourselves in a pickle, there's no mistake!' he said. 'But it's going to take more than One-Eyed Bart to outwit old Topaz, my purry, furry friend. I've been wracking my brains for a way out of this.'

So have I, thought Beancat. *It's why I'm here. I'm trying to come up with a plan, too.*

Captain Topaz picked up Beancat and popped her on his lap. She closed her eyes happily.

Not ten minutes had passed before the door to the captain's cabin swung open wide. Beancat's ears swivelled and she opened one of her big green eyes. (Don't be fooled by a 'half-asleep' cat. Though lazier than a ripe plum hanging from a tree with little more to do than take in all that sunshine, a cat can switch from light doze to being halfway up your best curtains in the swish of a tail.)

In walked two of Bart's crew. One was carrying a pewter plate with a hunk of bread and cheese on it and a pewter tankard of something. The other man held

a musket (which is a rifle with a trumpet-like end) pointed directly at Captain Topaz. Outside, the doorway was almost entirely blocked by the figure of Ten-Tun. They clearly weren't taking any chances that Captain Topaz might escape.

'I hope you're looking after my crew,' said Topaz.

'I'd worry about yourself, if I were you,' said the pirate holding the musket. He was wearing a red-and-white-striped bandana around his head like a sweat band.

Beancat jumped down from her master's lap in a lazy, almost slow-motion, don't-mind-me-it's-not-important, kind of way. She'd seen the cabin now and had an escape plan forming in her mind. She wandered past the two pirates, past the empty but locked treasure chest, past the globe and over to the doorway, making a point of rubbing against Ten-Tun's leg and looking up at him as she purred and left the room. It was all carefully done so the LAST thing anyone would think was, *This is a cat on a mission! We must stop her!*

Ten-Tun looked down and gave her an extra-special golden three-toothed grin.

'So that's where you got to, pretty lady,' he said, with that voice of his, as deep as a whale's.

Furry Purry Beancat meowed hello then, free once more, she went in search of One-Eyed Bart. She had a plan.

Beancat dashed here and there, hither and thither, port to starboard (that's left to right, for you land lubbers), starboard to port, bow to aft (that's front to back) and from aft to bow.

Suddenly, Beancat caught a glimpse of Captain One-Eyed Bart in his tricorn hat, standing by the main mast. *Aha!* she *thought. I've—*

'GOTCHA!' said a voice and an enormous paw landed on her beautiful tail. She tried to move but found that she was going nowhere. Something or someone had her tail in a very tight grip.

Beancat turned to face . . . to face . . . the biggest, meanest, most muscly moggy she'd ever seen in any of her lives. He had very few whiskers and those he did have were of uneven length. His fur was matted and uncared for. And he stank of pickled herring. But, by golly, he was handsome. There was no arguing the point there. He was one mighty, terrifying, ginger tomcat.

'You must be Furry Purry Beancat!' he sneered. 'The *tame* cat with a collar.'

Beancat had been aware that she was wearing a collar but had not thought much about it. She couldn't see it herself because, when she looked down, the fur from her furry, purry head and neck was in the way.

'Must be' Furry Purry Beancat? she thought. *He said 'must be'. That means we've not met before.*

'And who might you be?' she asked without so much as a hiss or a raising of hackles.

'Guess,' said the cat.

'The cook's cat aboard the *Doubloon*, living off leftovers?' she asked innocently. (In case you're wondering, Furry Purry Beancat was trying to sound MUCH braver than she actually felt.)

The cat bared his yellowing teeth and gave Beancat a blast of herring-breath.

'I'm Cannonball,' he said.

Cannonball is a very good name for you, thought Beancat. *It suits you. You look as solid and as dangerous as a cannonball. But I'm not going to admit that, now, am I?* Instead, she said: 'Cannonball? Is that because you're as round as a Christmas pudding? Have you ever considered exercise?'

Cannonball, cat-king of the *Doubloon,* arched his back in outrage and raised his paw to swipe his claws across this impertinent cat's face . . . which was precisely what Furry Purry Beancat was hoping he would do. Because the heavy paw he had been using to pin her tail to the deck was now free.

Cannonball's rising anger had been quicker than his thinking. The moment he lifted his paw, Beancat whooshed away and lost herself amongst Captain One-Eyed Bart's victorious crew, who were celebrating on the deck.

WHOOOOOOOOOOOOOOOOOOOOOOO OOOOOOOOOOOOOOOOOOSH!

The enormous ginger tom went to chase after her. One pounce and he'd have this feeble feminine feline! But he was in for a bit of a shock. A rude awakening. Now something was holding *him* back by *his* tail. He pulled forward and felt something yanking at it. The more he pulled, the tighter it got.

He turned.

A large one-eared rat with a very goofy expression was sitting a safe enough distance away, looking at him with crazy eyes.

'Ahoy!' said Morris.

Cannonball looked down at his ginger tail to see a piece of string attached to it halfway down. The other end of the string was tied, very neatly, to an iron ring set in a block of wood on the deck.

Cannonball looked at his tail.

The string.

The iron ring.

And then back again.

The knots were tiny and very tight. Exactly the kind of knots that could be tied by a tiny rat's nimble paws.

'I done that,' said Morris, nodding his goofy head as he grinned a ratty-toothed grin. 'I'm good at knots.'

Cannonball was not very happy. In fact, you could say he was the complete *opposite* of very happy. There was no WAY he could untie those knots with his great big, cat paws. He SNARLED and HISSED and ARCHED HIS BACK AGAIN. He wanted to explode with rage!

'You look very frightening,' said Morris. He was telling the truth but he didn't SOUND it, which made Cannonball angrier still. He twisted and leaped at the rat, which wasn't the smartest of moves.

Now he was in quite a tangle.

'Slip knot,' Morris told him. 'Gets tighter the more you pull. Like a hangman's moose.'

'Hangman's noose, Uncle!' laughed a

little rat poking its head up next to him.

'You goose!' cried another.

The seven little rats – all but their sister, Blue – seemed to appear from nowhere, scurrying over to their Uncle Morris.

'Hangman's goose!'

'Honk! Goosy honk!'

'Hangman's papoose!'

'Hangman's loose!'

'Loose knickers!' cried the youngest.

'KNICKERS!' chorused the naughty little rats.

'Noose,' said Uncle Morris. 'I meant noose!'

Cannonball wasn't listening. All he cared about was that he'd been outsmarted by a bunch of ship's rats who were now *laughing at him*. Back on the *Doubloon*, he prided himself on being an excellent rat-catcher and even those who did manage to escape were TERRIFIED of him. They never dared show their faces.

But here on the *Rapier?* The rats thought he was a JOKE.

Furry Purry Beancat, meanwhile, hadn't wasted so much as a second. She was making up for lost time. She had found One-Eyed Bart standing at the foot of the main mast next to a large, open-topped, half-empty barrel of rum.

His men kept walking past, leaning into the barrel and filling their tin mugs or pewter tankards, chipped china teacups or even in one case, half a coconut shell with drink. And each was sure to nod his head or grunt or say, 'Thanks, Captain,' in appreciation.

But Beancat wasn't interested in the crew and their free tots of rum. Her beautiful big, green cat eyes were firmly fixed on One-Eyed Bart's belt. From it hung a huge set of keys.

CHAPTER 5
THAT SINKING FEELING!

Those must be Captain Topaz's keys, thought Furry Purry Beancat. *The ones he said that Bart had taken . . . including the one I need if my plan is to succeed!*

She was crouching behind a pile of weapons which must have been removed

from the defeated crew of the *Rapier*. There was an assortment of cutlasses, swords, knives, clubs and even a wooden catapult.

'Ahoy there, Miss Beancat!'

Beancat looked down to see little Blue sitting in the shadow of a cutlass handle. She must have been there the whole time, but with all the sea air and gunpowder and rum and dirty, sweaty sailors about, Beancat hadn't picked up the little rat's scent.

'Blue! What are you doing here?' Beancat asked.

'I wanted to see the enemy close up!'

Beancat felt proud to have such brave and loyal friends aboard the *Rapier*,

but would they be enough to stop Bart from sinking it?

Distracted by Blue, the first thing Furry Purry Beancat knew about Ten-Tun's arrival on the scene was when he loomed over the pile of discarded weapons and picked her up. She switched into mega-purr mode and rubbed against his chest and chin.

'I thought you were guarding Topaz,' One-Eyed Bart snapped at Ten-Tun.

'I've come here for me rum, like you says I should, Captain,' said Ten-Tun. 'I've left Bowman and Scraggs guarding the door.'

'Fair enough,' said Bart.

Ten-Tun tickled Beancat under her chin.

I'm not surprised he left two men to take his place, she thought. *He takes up the space of two!*

'Captain, I were wonderin' . . .'

'Yes?' said Bart.

'Do you think the *Doubloon* could do with a second ship's cat?'

One-Eyed Bart looked at Beancat. He saw her beautiful fur. He heard her beautiful purr. 'I'm not sure Cannonball would like it,' he said.

'But I don't want to leave her behind,' said Ten-Tun. 'She's too pretty and purry and furry to let her drown when we sinks the ship.'

That's nice of him, thought Beancat, *but it would be even nicer if he didn't*

*want them to sink the ship at all! The
sooner we rescue Captain Topaz the
better!*

From the safety and vantage point of
Ten-Tun's arms, Furry Purry Beancat was
able to get a close look at *her* captain's
keys hanging from the large, metal ring
around *another* pirate captain's belt.
Humph.

There was one particularly large,
particularly ornate key that looked to
her like it matched the fancy patterned
metalwork on the treasure chest.

That must be the key to the chest, she
thought.

It was a very nice key.

A beautifully carved key.

A very desirable must-have key and Furry Purry Beancat MUST HAVE IT! But how?

She looked down at the pile of weapons, and spotted her own reflection in one of the captured swords lying on the deck. The metal hadn't been that shiny, but it was just shiny enough for her to make out her head and see the collar Cannonball had been so rude about. It was a velvety midnight blue and appeared to be studded with . . . could those be *rubies*? Surely not.

The key.

Her collar.

And now her rescue plan was fully formed.

She jumped from Ten-Tun's arms and jerked her head at Blue who was still sitting in the pile of weapons, indicating that the little rat should follow her. They had work to do . . .

One-Eyed Bart had returned to his ship to sleep off his victory celebrations, but left behind many of his crew to keep guard. Furry Purry Beancat gathered the rats in a corner of the hold, where the crew of the *Rapier* were being held prisoner in almost total darkness.

Some of the pirates were sitting or sprawling on the floor. Some were asleep

on their feet, leaning against a fellow prisoner. All of them were tied up with rope. A sliver of silver moonlight found its way through a gap between the hatch and the deck high above, slicing through the blackness.

Ethel had been in a terrible state ever since Beancat had told the rats what One-Eyed Bart had planned for the ship.

'What a nasty, evil, horrible man,' she said. 'Going to drown us all like that!'

'Don't worry, my love,' said Gordon. 'Beancat has a plan!'

'I do,' said Furry Purry Beancat, 'but I need your family's help.'

'What is it, Miss Beancat?' asked Blue.

'There is no way Captain Topaz can get

out of the cabin with Ten-Tun on guard and, even if there was a huge distraction, I don't think Ten-Tun would leave his post unguarded,' she said. 'He made sure he had two men in his place when he went for his tot of rum.'

'So, we're going bash him on the head!' said an excited young rat.

'Biff him on the bonce!'

'Punch him on the nose!'

'Nibbles his toes!'

'Knobble his knees!'

'Nibble his knobbly knees!'

'Batter his bu—'

'QUIET, CHILDREN!' snapped their mother.

'So-rry, Mamma,' they all said as one.

'Go on, Beancat,' said Gordon.

'What do you think Bart's men would do if they opened the captain's cabin door and found him gone?' she asked.

'They'd search the room!'

'What if he wasn't there?'

'Then they'd search the ship!' said Blue.

'Hunt high and low!' said a brother.

'Hunt low and high!' said a sister.

'From port to starboard!'

'From starboard to port!'

'From top to bottom!'

'They'd search under everyone's BOTTOM!' squealed one in delight.

Uncle Morris gave a goofy laugh.

Gordon *shhh*-ed them again.

'So-rry, Dad!' they all said in unison.

'Exactly,' said Furry Purry Beancat. 'They'd abandon the empty cabin and go in search of the missing Captain Topaz.'

'But how can we make him disappear?' asked Ethel.

'I'll tell you,' said Furry Purry Beancat, and explained it all extremely carefully.

When she had finished, Gordon was very impressed.

'I'm very impressed,' said Gordon.

'Right,' said Furry Purry Beancat. Her heart was beating a little faster in that furry, purry chest of hers, a mixture of excitement and fear. There was a lot of derring-do to be done in all this danger! 'There's no time to lose!'

Ethel and Gordon's family began to take it in turns to nibble through the ropes which tied Powder Monkey's hands together. Once he was free, he'd be able to untie his own legs and then start untying the other members of Captain Topaz's crew who, in turn, could untie others too, and so on.

'Why don't we all chew through the other pirates' ropes at the same time, Dad?' asked one little rat.

'Nibble!'

'Gnaw!'

'Lend a paw!'

'Bite!'

'Eat!'

'Lend a feet!'

There was more giggling.

'We can't speak Human and they can't speak Animal,' Gordon told them. 'Which means we can't EXPLAIN what we're doing so they might think we're trying to eat them!'

'But Powder Monkey won't think that,' Ethel explained, 'because he's a friend!'

Furry Purry Beancat and Blue, meanwhile, were off on the main mission: to find Captain One-Eyed Bart whom they'd last seen going back aboard his own ship, the *Doubloon*.

Slinking through the dark, the cat and the rat made their way past the spot where Cannonball's tail had been tied to the iron ring with string. The ring was still there with the string attached to it but there was no sign of Cannonball or his tail, except for a few ginger hairs.

'Uh-oh,' said Blue. 'That nasty cat is on the loose again!'

'Hopefully he'll be hunting rats not us,' said Furry Purry Beancat without thinking. She saw Blue's expression. 'I mean, back on the *Doubloon* . . . and,

anyway,' she added hurriedly, 'you *Rapier* rats are far too smart to let any old ginger tom catch them!'

They reached one of the planks lashing the two ships together. Fluffy tail held high and with a proud look on her face (cats are SO good at proud, I-know-something-you-don't faces) Beancat sauntered over to the deck of the *Doubloon*.

Blue had rather a different approach. She scampered across very quickly on the UNDERSIDE of the plank, running upside down like only rodents can!

'Nicely done,' said Beancat when Blue joined her.

The layout of most ships is very similar, if not exactly the same, so they found Bart's captain's cabin soon enough and, it being a balmy night, luckily Bart had left the door wide open to let in some air. (And, I should explain, that's balmy as in warm and not barmy as in . . . well, a bit like Uncle Morris.)

Now, I suppose I should let you in on this stage of Furry Purry Beancat's plan. It was quite simply to:

🐱 get the ring of keys off Bart's belt
🐱 take the treasure-chest key off the ring of keys

116

🐾 put the ring of keys (minus the treasure-chest key) back on his belt

🐾 leave with the treasure-chest key

See? Nothing to it.

Except that it had to be done without waking One-Eyed Bart. And Blue and Beancat had paws rather than hands! This meant that, simple though the idea might be, carrying it out for real would be rather more difficult.

No wonder Beancat and Blue were n-n-n-nervous.

CHAPTER 6
THE KEY TO SUCCESS!

Bart wasn't asleep in his berth but, in good old pirate-captain-after-a-victory tradition, he was asleep, fully-clothed in a chair, a leather bottle still somehow clasped in his hand. He was snoring in good old pirate-captain tradition too – by which I mean loud enough to out-snore even the

gruntiest of grunty pigs. He smelled of rum and sweat and gunpowder.

Beancat looked at the keyring on his belt. The keyring was just that: a great big iron ring. It was nothing like a keyring you can fit in your pocket with the house keys. Neither the ring nor a single key on it could fit in any pocket. These were BIG keys.

The iron keyring wasn't a complete circle, though. It had a small gap in it, so that keys could be slipped on or off – added or taken away.

This was also the way that Beancat hoped they'd get the keyring off the belt. There was no way either of them could simply undo Bart's belt-buckle and slip off the ring that way. Cat's paws, rat's paws and combined teeth wouldn't be strong enough to achieve that small miracle.

When Beancat had been up on deck – when Ten-Tun had picked her up and asked Bart if they could save her from the sinking – she had been studying those keys, studying that ring and studying this belt as the plan was taking shape in her mind.

Following Beancat's instructions, Blue scuttled up the side of the chair and on to sleeping Bart's lap. Very slowly, very carefully, the rat turned the ring in her tiny paws so that the gap lined up with the edge of the pirate captain's belt.

Having positioned herself on the arm of the chair, Furry Purry Beancat now, ever so gingerly (despite being tabby and white), slid a white front paw under the belt, against Bart's tummy, so that Blue could work the ring off more easily.

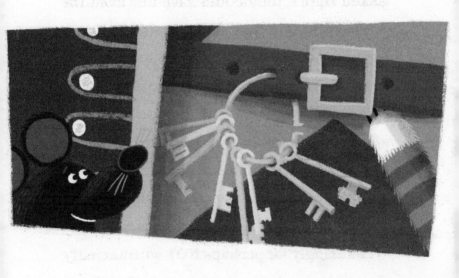

The result was rather *too* successful. The ring, and all the keys, fell on to Bart's

lap – narrowly missing the little black rat – and slid on to the floor of his cabin with a clatter.

In the still of the night, with just the gentle lapping of the water against the side of the ships and the creaking of the rigging, the noise sounded loud enough to wake the dead. Furry Purry Beancat half-expected three ghosts and a skeleton to come in and ask them to keep the noise down. She jumped down to hide underneath the chair before you could say, '*I-don't-want-this-plan-ruined-before-it's-even-started!*'

Amazingly, or perhaps NOT so amazingly if you knew how much drink One-Eyed Bart had drunk (and drinking the kind of drinks he'd been drinking made him very drunk), the enemy captain wasn't woken by the sound. Instead he just threw his arms around a little, shifted his position in the chair a little, shouted, 'PEACHES!' then started snoring again.

Blue scurried down the side of the chair and joined Beancat on the floor of the cabin.

The fall had caused two of the eight keys to come off the ring. And they were in luck. One of them was the key to Captain Topaz's empty treasure chest!

Yippee! thought Furry Purry Beancat. *We need every piece of luck we can get, however small!*

With a few attempts and much effort, Blue managed to get the key in her mouth – looking quite like a very small rat-like dog with a very large metal bone. There was no way Blue could carry the key for more than a moment or two, it was too big and too heavy so, as Beancat had planned beforehand, the little rat pushed it behind Furry Purry Beancat's collar. Now Beancat's neck is VERY FURRY INDEED, so she looked extremely comical with the key sticking through the ruff of fluff!

So far so good.

But now they realized that they couldn't

put the ring with the remaining keys back on Bart's belt. They'd have to leave it on the floor and hope when Bart woke up he'd just think it had fallen off.

Blue had never been so excited in all her life. 'Now all you have to do is give the key to Captain Topaz!' she said, as they made their way out of the cabin.

Of course, 'all you have to do' wasn't really true. When you're a cat and you're giving a key to a human, the hardest part of the plan is TRYING TO EXPLAIN WHAT YOU WANT HIM TO DO WITH IT.

Furry Purry Beancat and Blue reached Captain Topaz's cabin to find it being guarded by two pirates whom Beancat took to be Scraggs and Bowman, the men Ten-Tun had spoken about earlier. The giant himself was nowhere to be seen.

'You get back to your mother and father now,' said Beancat, turning to the little rat. 'And, Blue?'

'Yes, Miss Beancat?'

'You were AMAZING. They should be very proud of you.'

Blue gave an excited little ratty squeak. 'Thank you!' she said, and disappeared into the night.

Now Furry Purry Beancat waited.

And waited.

And waited.

And waited . . .

. . . until, finally a man approached the door. He was wearing a yellow neckerchief.

'What do you want?' asked one of the men on guard.

'Telescope, Scraggs,' said Yellow Neckerchief. 'First Mate wants Topaz's telescope.'

'This time of night?' said Scraggs.

'He says it's a very fine brass and leather one,' said Yellow Neckerchief. 'Expect he wants it before someone else gets the idea to have it for himself!'

'Ain't that the truth,' said Scraggs.

'Just our luck to be on guard duty,' said

Bowman. 'I thought we'd be a-drinkin' and celebratin' with the rest of the crew, yet we're stuck here. It just ain't fair.'

'So quit bein' a pirate and join the Royal Navy!' laughed Yellow Neckerchief. 'I hear they're equally strict with everyone!'

Bowman and Scraggs laughed and stood aside. Yellow Neckerchief opened the door, went into the cabin and closed it. Scraggs and Bowman blocked the door once more.

Beancat crept forward in that slow-motion way that only a cat on the prowl can. She was positioned and ready. She couldn't do her usual dash because the key might fall from her collar and all would be lost. But she still had to be quick.

The door opened, and Yellow Neckerchief

came out, holding a brass telescope in a leather case.

As quick as a slightly-more-cautious-flash-than-usual, Furry Purry Beancat nipped past him and into the cabin.

'What was th—' Bowman said.

'Only Topaz's cat,' she heard Scraggs say, as the door was slammed behind her.

'Ah, THERE you are, Furry Purry Beancat!' said the captain from behind his desk, his face breaking into a most contented smile. 'I thought you'd abandoned me!'

Beancat gave a friendly meow and jumped up on to the map spread out before him.

When she landed, the key fell from her collar with a clunk.

The captain rubbed Beancat between the ears before lifting up the key. Here was a human who got his priorities right – looking after Beancat came first.

'What have we here?' he wondered. 'Why, it's the key to my treasure chest . . . If only you could talk, Beancat! You could tell me who tucked it in your collar and what they thought I might do with it. Clean my ears?' He stuck the key in one ear and made a funny face.

If I could talk, thought Beancat, *I could tell you that it was a young rat who put it there. I wonder what you'd think of that?*

In one leap, Furry Purry Beancat made it from the desk to the treasure chest. The lid was curved and very shiny, so she

ended in a scrabbling of paws to maintain her dignity, her claws making a *clickety-clack* sound on the wood

'It's empty and not much use to me,' said the captain. 'There's no gold inside to use to bribe the guards.'

'*Hide inside it! Hide inside it! Hide inside it!*' Beancat meowed.

The captain got up and came over to the treasure chest, key in hand. 'What's got into you? I told you there's nothing inside.'

'*Hide inside it! Hide inside it! Hide inside it!*'

'Fine. I'll show you,' the captain said, and turned the key in the lock. He lifted the curved lid on well-oiled hinges. 'Look,' he showed Beancat. 'Empty!'

Beancat jumped straight into the chest and meowed.

Captain Topaz leaned inside and began to lift her out. Then he stopped. 'Do you know what . . .' He lowered his voice. 'This trunk is big enough for me to hide inside!'

Precisely, thought Beancat. She purred even louder and it was further amplified by the walls of the trunk. *They know the trunk is locked so they'll never dream that you're inside it. Open the widow. Hide in the trunk*

and they'll think you've escaped. Hide in the trunk!

The captain lifted out Furry Purry Beancat and placed her on the floor.

'Do you know what, Beancat?' he said. 'You've given me an idea.'

Yes, yes, yes! thought Beancat. *Hide in the trunk. They'll search the room, find you gone and run off in panic, leaving the door open. Do it!*

She was already planning her next part of the plan. If the captain left the window open before hiding, she would stand beneath it yowling. If he simply hid in the trunk, as though he'd disappeared into thin air, she would sit in the middle of the floor of the cabin, trembling, and staring saucer-eyed at n-n-nothing as if she'd seen a ghost.

The captain grinned. 'Do you know what, I could hide inside this trunk—' he began just when Furry Purry Beancat heard the door to the captain's cabin opening.

NO!!! Not now!

Captain Topaz quickly closed the lid. Her plan would be ruined.

In came Scraggs, closely followed by Bowman. Bowman was holding a blunderbuss. He pointed it straight at the captain.

'We was thinkin',' said Scraggs.

'Yeah,' said Bowman. 'Thinkin'.'

'We was thinkin that it ain't right everyone else is havin' a good time or sleepin'—'

'Ain't right,' said Bowman, his weapon still pointing straight at the captain's head.

'While us two is stuck here havin' to guard you,' said Scraggs.

'And we didn't even get no telescope,' said Bowman.

'That's not very fair, is it, gentlemen?' said the captain. He gave the blunderbuss about as much attention as a buttercup. 'But you've come at just the right time, if it's booty you're after.'

'Booties?' said Bowman. 'What would I do with booties?' He looked down at his feet.

'Not booties,' Scraggs snapped. 'Booty. Plunder. TREASURE!'

'Precisely,' said the captain, with a nod.

'You know what this is, don't you, gentlemen?'

''Course we do,' said Bowman. 'It's a chest.'

'What kind of chest?' asked the captain.

'TREASURE CHEST!' said Scraggs and Bowman.

'Correct,' said the captain. 'And what if I were to give you a few trinkets? Say, a handful of gold coins and a few diamond necklaces each?'

'Why don't I just shoot you and we keep everything for ourselves?' said Bowman.

'You could do that,' said the captain, with a shrug. 'But are you really brave enough to face up to Captain One-Eyed Bart? I doubt he'd be happy if you did it without orders from him.'

'Which is why we ain't going to do that,' said Scraggs hurriedly. 'But what would you want in return for the gold and necklaces? We ain't gonna let you go.'

'Heaven forbid, no,' said the captain. 'I couldn't ask an honest pair of pirates like you to double-cross your captain.'

'Then what?' asked Scraggs

'Yeah, what?' asked Bowman.

Yes, what are you playing at? Beancat wondered.

'I'm hungry and I'm sure my cat is hungry too. Who knows what your captain has in store for me?'

'He'll think o' somethin' nice an' nasty,' Bowman began, only to be jabbed in the stomach with Scraggs's elbow.

'Who knows?' said Scraggs.

'So I was hoping you could make things as comfortable for me as possible in here. Some food for me and my cat. Some wine. A lantern—'

'No lantern, said Scraggs. 'If you set fire to the ship, we'll be in trouble. And, anyhows, it's a moonlit night and them there windows is big!'

'Fair enough,' said the captain. 'No lantern. But the rest?'

Bowman prodded him in the shoulder with the end of the blunderbuss. 'Show us the gold first,' he said. 'Then we'll decide.'

'Yeah, that's right,' said Scraggs. 'We need to see the treasure first.'

'Very well,' said the captain. He carefully lifted Furry Purry Beancat off the lid of the treasure chest and plonked her on his desk, just to the left of Bowman and his blunderbuss. 'There you go, Scratchy Bitey Beancat,' he said in a quiet, soothing voice. 'You behave for me.'

What did her beloved Captain Topaz just call her? Did he just say Scratchy Bitey Beancat? Was he trying to ask her to behave in a particular way? What was he up to . . .?

Beancat got ready to pounce.

Captain Topaz crouched down in front of his treasure chest, the key still in the lock.

He started to lift the lid.

'No. Wait!' said Scraggs. 'Let me do that.'

He lifted the lid, the expression on his face turning from excitement to disappointment in the blink of an eye.

'What is this?' snarled Scraggs. 'A trick?'

The chest was as empty as a cuckoo's nest!

Bowman looked FURIOUS. 'Tell me why I shouldn't blow your head off right now!'

'Gentlemen, wait!' said the captain. 'A false bottom! This treasure chest has a false bottom. There's a whole extra layer of treasure under it. Let me show you.'

Still crouching, he leaned inside, stretching out his hand.

'No, wait!' said Scraggs, a second time.

'Leave both hands where we can see them. I'll find this false bottom.'

'If you say so,' said the captain, still crouching.

Scraggs leaned forward into the chest. Before he knew what was happening, Captain Topaz was bringing the heavy lid down on his head with one hand while, at the same time, turning towards Bowman who, momentarily startled, had been slow to pull the blunderbuss's trigger.

As the captain turned, the woodworm-riddled stool leg came flying out of his sleeve where he had hidden it. It hurtled towards Bowman.

But missed.

There was a blast from the blunderbuss.

CHAPTER 7
THE TIDE TURNS

Fortunately for Captain Topaz, the blunderbuss also missed its target. This was because not only could Bowman not see the captain but he was also in a lot of pain. He currently had a Scratchy Bitey Beancat wrapped around the front of his head. She smelled rather nicely of warm cat – Furry Purry Beancat has a very nice smell – but he was too distracted by the screaming pain from her claws in the back of his head, and not being able to see. And, oh, yes, by her biting his nose.

He was trying to shout, 'Get this cat off me! Get it off me!' but, with a face full of Scratchy Bitey Beancat's furry tummy, it came out as meaningless muffled sounds.

Not that Scraggs could have helped him. He was currently out cold, half-in and half-out of an empty treasure chest with no false bottom, having been knocked out by the lid.

The captain quickly overpowered Bowman.

Beancat decided that it was time to let go of her prey. Bowman looked almost grateful to be tied to a chair with his own trousers. She jumped to the cabin floor and, as *Furry Purry* Beancat once more, began washing her paws.

Of the two, Scraggs was nearer the captain's size than Bowman was, so it was Scraggs's clothes that the captain put on to disguise himself (which was fortunate because Bowman's trousers had already been put to good use).

'I don't know what the plan was for whoever put that key in your collar, Beancat,' he said, as he made a few last-

minute alterations to his disguise, 'but it worked out rather well, don't you agree?'

Furry Purry Beancat *purrrrrrrrrrrrred*.

That was me, she thought. *Me and some VERY special rats.*

'You are the cleverest of cats!' said the pirate captain. 'Now all I have to do is get Bart and his crew off my ship!' He made it sound simple, like going for a row or burying some treasure.

The sinking! thought Furry Purry Beancat. *You've got to stop the sinking!*

'I can't take you out of the cabin with me,' said the captain sadly. 'I've gone to all this trouble to look like a deckhand and carrying such a beautiful girl as you would be BOUND to attract attention.'

Not only are you right, thought Beancat, *but you explained it perfectly.*

Rather than carefully opening the door first, and peering outside to check the coast was clear, the disguised captain Topaz opened the door to his cabin and strode out like someone who had every right to be doing that: one of One-Eyed Bart's victorious crew. That's why he was the *captain*.

Furry Purry Beancat dashed ahead. She went straight to the hold to find out how successful or not Gordon and his family had been at freeing the crew. She found that those *Rapier* pirates who'd already been untied were busy untying the others.

'You did it!' said Beancat when she

spotted Gordon.

'What about you?' asked Gordon. 'Did you free the captain?'

'Not quite as planned,' Beancat admitted. 'But he's free!'

'That's grand!' said Gordon. He sounded happier than she'd ever heard him since waking up on the pirate captain's hat! 'Me boys and girls bit through Powder Monkey's bonds like they was butter and —'

Ethel appeared in the shaft of moonlight. 'You're safe!' she said to Beancat, looking around. 'Where's the captain?'

'He's free,' said Furry Purry Beancat. 'I'm sure he'll find us soon.'

'Good,' said Ethel. She sounded worried as always. 'This lot may be untied but they need telling what to do. You should hear some of the hare-brained schemes they've come up with! They need their captain or they'll all end up prisoners again . . . or maybe even worse.'

They were looking between the ever-increasing forest of legs, as more and more of the *Rapier* crew were stretching their limbs after hours of captivity.

'Where are the kids?' Gordon asked Ethel.

'With you,' said Ethel.

'If they was with me, I wouldn't be asking where they was,' said Gordon. 'I thought they was with you?'

'No,' said Ethel.

'They're probably with Uncle Morris,'

said Beancat. 'I'm sure they'll be f—'

'They're not with Morris,' said Gordon. 'He went off in search of Cannonball.'

'Has Morris *seen* Cannonball?' asked Beancat. 'He's an enormous fighting machine!'

'It was him what tied his tail to that iron ring and saved your furry skin last time around,' said Ethel. 'He's brave, I'll give him that.'

'He's silly, is what he is!' said Gordon.

He's probably a bit of both, thought Furry Purry Beancat but she was far too polite to say anything.

'Where are my babies?' wailed Ethel. 'They shouldn't be running around in this chaos!'

'We're rats on a ship, Mamma,' said Blue, appearing out of the darkness. 'You've nothing to worry about.'

'Apart from that big bad cat,' said one of her brothers, appearing from behind her.

'And knives!' said another.

'And swords!' They all came tumbling into view, clambering over each other.

'And pistols!'

'And drowning. We should all worry about drowning!'

'That's QUITE enough of that, thank you!' said Ethel, greatly relieved and back in stern-mother mode.

'So-rry, Mamma!' said the mischievous little rats, not sounding sorry at all!

'Sssh!' said Gordon. 'I smell the captain.'

A murmur went up amongst the pirates as Captain Topaz appeared in the hold. A feeling of relief spread around the room. They probably would have cheered if they hadn't had to keep quiet.

'Listen up, my motley crew!' Captain Topaz hissed. 'We've let this occupation go on long enough! It's time to take back control of the *Rapier* from these interlopers!'

'Inter-whaters, Cap'n?' asked First Mate Muggins, clutching his hideous monkey-mermaid charm.

'Invaders!' said Captain Topaz.

Muggins nodded with approval. He knew what invaders were. 'We're to repel all boarders!' he said.

Furry Purry Beancat STILL didn't know what that meant!

'I think we should give the captain and crew all the help they can get, don't you?' she said to the rats.

'You're right! The battle ain't over till it's over,' said Gordon, which sounded very impressive and brave in that treacly voice of his, until he added, 'Or something like that . . . Anyway, I've rounded up the rats from the other ship and they're quite an army! They hate Cannonball the rat-catcher and they hate his master, One-Eyed Bart. They're MORE than happy to fight alongside us to defend this 'ere ship!'

'You have been busy,' said Beancat. She was extremely impressed with her friend Gordon.

'That's a great, Dad!' said Blue.

'Not you, Blue,' said Gordon. 'I can't have you fighting. I need you to keep your brothers and sisters safe.'

Furry Purry Beancat could see that Blue was disappointed, but the little rat seemed to understand that what her father said made sense. She was even more proud when Gordon lowered his voice and said, 'You're the littlest and the youngest but the brightest and the bravest, Blue, which is why I've put YOU in charge.'

'Fighting humans is like playing with

fire,' piped up Ethel.

'And playing with fire is most *dangerous*,' said one of the little rats. 'You could get burned!'

'Fried like an egg!'

'Grilled like a kipper!'

'Roasted like an ox!'

'Boiled like a . . .'

'. . . boiled thing!'

They fell about laughing.

'Shh-afety fir-sht!' said Uncle Morris, who suddenly rolled into view across the floor of the hold. 'I fell in the barrel of grog!' he said, and laughed, then had an attack of the hiccups and rolled away.

Ethel tried to be angry with Morris but was clearly relieved that he'd come back in one piece.

He rolled back into view, giggling. 'What's the difference between an octopus and an old boot?' he asked.

'What are you on about, Morris?' asked Ethel.

'What's the difference between an octopus and an old boot?' Morris repeated.

'We're busy, Morris,' said Gordon. 'This is important. We're makin' plans.'

'It's a riddle! Ask me. Go on. What's the difference between an octopus and an old boot?'

'I don't know,' said Furry Purry Beancat. 'What IS the difference between an octopus and an old boot?'

Morris frowned.

He hiccupped. *HIC!*

He burped. *BURP!*

'How should I know?' he said, then rolled
away again. '*Weeeeeeeeeeee!*'

CHAPTER 8
A MIGHTY SPLASH!

The Battle for the *Rapier*, as the fight became known in pirate folklore, was one of the strangest battles in pirate history, which is why it is still remembered to this day. Most fights involving pirate ships were between pirate and naval ships, or between pirate and merchant ships trying to defend themselves. Less frequently, there were fights between two pirate ships or even pirate crews turning against their captains. But what makes The Battle for the *Rapier* so very, very special is that there is no record of any other such battle where the ships' rats TOOK SIDES.

Because, in The Battle for the *Rapier*, the rats fought alongside Captain Topaz's crew. So, as well as pirate-to-pirate combat, there was teeth-to-ankle combat too!

Captain One-Eyed Bart and his crew didn't stand a chance. Along with the element of surprise that the *Rapier* crew were suddenly free, many of Bart's crew were groggy from . . . well, too much grog, so not at their fighting best. Add in the fact

that Captain Topaz and his crew were fired up to regain what was (sort of) rightfully theirs – they were still pirates, remember – and that the decks were swarming with sharp-toothed rats who were only attacking pirates from the *Doubloon* crew, and it was hardly surprising that the *Rapier* was soon back under Captain Topaz's control.

Was the rat attack witchcraft?

Sorcery?

Nature gone mad?

Well, no. *We* know it was all a part of Furry Purry Beancat's plan. But the pirates didn't know that, did they?

And, although Captain Topaz's victory is still spoken of today, what isn't widely known is that Captain One-Eyed Bart's fall into the sea, near the start of the battle, wasn't because of a shot from a flintlock pistol or a well-aimed blow. No, the cause of Bart's early bath was a trip over a perfectly placed ankle-height piece of string tied from one side of the deck to the other. To be even more accurate, it wasn't a single piece of string but many small pieces of string, tied together with tiny knots.

Because while Blue may not have been allowed to fight, her paws hadn't been idle. She made the tripwire with the help of her seven VERY excited brothers and sisters.

'We might catch an elephant!'

'We could make a kite!'

'We could FIGHT a kite!'

'We could bite a kite!'

'We could bite an elephant!'

'Elephant steeeeew!'

'Elephant POOOOOOO!'

They thought that was the funniest thing in the world.

'Less talking, more knot-tying!' Blue insisted.

'So-rry, Blue!' they said together, in that sing song chorus of theirs, then laughed some more, but their nimble little ratty paws never stopped working.

When it was done, they tied it in place, so the string was as tight as could be, then the eight little rats hid in a coil of rope and watched and waited, with the noises of fighting all around them. They couldn't believe their luck when One-Eyed Bart –

the enemy captain himself – was their very first victim!

Bart was in a swordfight with Captain Topaz who was forcing him backwards across the deck, hacking swords.

THWACK!
CLASH!
CLINK!
THUNK!

They grunted. **GRUNT!**

They snarled. **SNARL!**

Then Captain One-Eyed Bart, one of the most feared men ever to have sailed the seven seas, tripped on the string, and fell backwards, hitting the top of the balustrade, and flipped over the rail straight into the sea.

Powder Monkey, who was standing next to Captain Topaz, reloading the captain's flintlock pistols as soon as he'd fired them and handing them back to him ready to fire again, witnessed the whole thing. He whooped for joy and LAUGHED!

As for the *Rapier's* own first mate, Muggins, he was shot at very close range with a flintlock pistol but walked away with hardly a scratch. This surprised him at first, though not as much as it surprised Seasalt, the enemy pirate who'd shot him!

'Witchcraft!' Seasalt cried, his eyes widening and jaw dropping.

When Muggins reached inside his shirt and pulled out the object that had saved him from the shot, Seasalt dropped his pistol, turned and ran. It was a hideously deformed, tar-coated, ugly, ugly, ugly miniature mermaid now peppered with gun pellets.

Accompanied by a ghastly smell.

Seasalt jumped over the side to join his captain in the water. Anywhere seemed safer than on board.

Muggins hugged his good-luck charm. It had worked!

At this point, Furry Purry Beancat had slunk away from the fighting. She had noticed one of One-Eyed Bart's crew was missing and had left a big gap: a single person but a very BIG part of the crew. It was Ten-Tun. She set off in search of him.

She found him, at last, in the bowels

of the *Rapier* – the part of the ship that sat below the surface the sea – far from the battle up above. But Ten-Tun was no coward. He wasn't hiding. He had a huge metal spike in one hand and an enormous wooden mallet in the other.

Furry Purry Beancat looked at the spike.

Furry Purry Beancat looked at the mallet.

And she knew that Ten-Tun had been sent to hole the ship: to hammer holes in the sides and bottom, to let the water in until, in time, the ship would sink completely. But he'd yet to hammer a single hole.

What's stopping him? Furry Purry Beancat wondered.

She jumped elegantly over to him and, purring as loudly as a lion, began to weave around his legs, her soft fur rubbing against his skin, her purrs vibrating through his body.

Puuuuuuuuuuuurrrrrrrrrrrrrrrrrrrr.

Ten-Tun dropped the mallet and fell to his knees. He put down the spike and held his head in his hands.

'I can't do it, pussycat,' he said. 'I can't do it. I wanted Captain Bart to let me take you with me so you'd be safe, but then I thought of all the people. Yes, I'd be saving you, my beautiful, fluffy Mistress Moggy, but letting your fellow crew drown!'

Furry Purry Beancat pushed her nose against his hands and nuzzled them.

'Captain Bart's looked after me since

I were a lad. I ain't got no parents of me own,' he whispered. 'I'm loyal and I'll give me life for him, but think of all the families who'll lose loved ones if I do this dreadful deed . . .'

He began to stroke Furry Purry Beancat's head. He looked deeply into her big, green eyes.

'It's different when you're fighting hand to hand, one to one – or one to three, because I like a fair fight 'cos I'm bigger than most,' said Ten-Tun, 'but sinking a ship when the crew don't even know it's happening? It's wrong.'

He sat down on the hull with a *bump* and Furry Purry Beancat hopped into his lap and he stroked her. And, as he stroked her, he became calmer and so did Furry Purry Beancat.

You can't beat stroking a furry purry cat, she thought. *And you're a good man at heart, Tommy Ten-Tun.*

The fight was over before dawn broke and the moonlight was replaced with the early morning sun. Captain Topaz was as puzzled as anyone about how his ship's rats had come to help them and how there were so many of them. Little did he know that their ranks had been swelled by those from Bart's ship. He ordered three sacks of grain to be brought up and placed on deck. He slashed it with his sword. 'A feast for our heroic friends!' he declared, and his crew cheered.

And which rat was the first to scurry forward to have a feed? It was Uncle Morris, of course!

'I'm hungry after all that fighting!' he said. In truth, Morris had quite a headache from too much grog and had spent most of the time fighting a discarded glove which he took to be an enemy spy. Early on in their fight, the glove had somehow been winning.

The captain then made a speech, with a special mention to his beloved Furry Purry Beancat who had brought him the all-important treasure-chest key in her collar.

Furry Purry Beancat just purred.

'What happens now?' asked Ethel later that evening, as the summer sun was beginning

to fade. They weren't hiding in the shadows any more, but up on deck enjoying the sea air.

'Bart and his crew sail away, weaponless and treasureless,' said Gordon.

'What about Cannonball?' asked Blue.

'I suspect he'll be more – er – polite to any rats he meets in the future,' said her father.

'I should hope so too,' said Furry Purry Beancat. 'Manners are very important to cats.' She gave an enormous yawn.

'What precisely did Uncle Morris do to Cannonball?' asked little Blue.

'Your uncle doesn't remember what he did or how,' said Gordon, 'but the last I saw of Cannonball, that beast of a cat was running around tangled up in a homemade net!'

'So *that's* what happened to the rest of the string,' squeaked Blue. 'Good old Uncle Morris!'

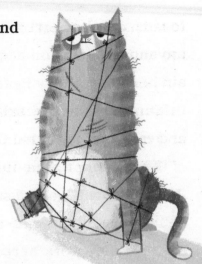

'Good old Uncle Morris,' agreed Gordon. 'You can never have too much string.'

Furry Purry Beancat was sleepy now. It had been a long night. She thought of Captain Topaz, back in charge of the ship as he should be. At that precise moment, plotting a course on the charts in his cabin, the captain thought of Furry Purry Beancat too and smiled.

Then Furry Purry Beancat found herself thinking of Tommy Ten-Tun, a good man at heart and, just then, over on the deck of the *Doubloon*, Ten-Tun thought of Furry Purry Beancat too and smiled.

'I think I'll have a cat nap,' Beancat declared. 'My work here is done.'

'Sleep well, Miss Beancat,' said Blue.

'You too, Blue,' said Furry Purry Beancat. 'You too.'

Furry Purry Beancat found a patch of sunlight, followed her tail around in a circle three times, then settled herself down in a furry ball of purry cat. She yawned, lowered her head to the ground and pulled her beautiful, fluffy tail in front of her little pink nose.

Where will I wake up next? she wondered, slowly closing her big green eyes and drifting off to sleep . . .

PHILIP ARDAGH

Roald Dahl-Funny-Prize-winning author
PHILIP ARDAGH has been published
for around thirty years, written more
than 100 titles and been translated into
forty languages. Books range from his
bestselling and international award-
winning *Eddie Dickens adventures* —
celebrating twenty years in 2020 — to
his prize-winning *Grubtown Tales*, the
Grunt series, illustrated by Axel Scheffler,
and *High in the Clouds*, a collaboration
with Sir Paul McCartney, currently
being developed as a film by Netflix.

ROB BIDDULPH is a bestselling and multi award-winning author/illustrator and the official World Book Day Illustrator for 2020. His first picture book, *Blown Away*, won the Waterstones Children's Book Prize in 2015. His second book, *GRRRRR!* was nominated for the CILIP Greenaway Medal and the IBW Children's Picture Book of the Year in 2016.

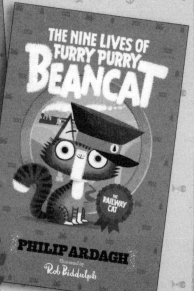

THE NINE LIVES OF
FURRY PURRY
BEANCAT

THE
LIBRARY
CAT

PHILIP ARDAGH

Illustrated by
Rob Biddulph

COMING
SOON!

THE REAL

FURRY PURRY BEANCAT

PHILIP ARDAGH didn't have a pet as a child, except when looking after the class tadpole one weekend. He was in his twenties when he got his very first pet, a long-haired tabby-and-white cat called Beany. 'I loved her to bits!' he said. 'She was very furry and very purry!' Beany lived into her eighteenth year and, in creaky old age, sat with Philip in his study as he wrote. One day, it occurred to him that – if he slightly skewed the meaning of a cat having nine lives – she could have eight other exciting lives . . . and the idea of **THE NINE LIVES OF PURRY FURRY BEANCAT** was born.